Copyright 2014 by Jill Telford

All rights reserved, including the right to reproduce this book or portions thereof in any form whatsoever.

ISBN 978-1494994907
ISBN 1494994909

Fly Away Publishing 2014

For more information on special discounts and readings please contact the author by email: jill.telford@gmail.com

I woke up and started writing. God this is what it would be like if Heaven had a mailbox.

Dedicated to everyone who lived and to everyone who died. Especially to all the angels flying invisibly around us.

Part One:

I opened my closet door that stored stacked suitcases one on top of the other. I pulled out the blue worn suitcase by the handle while steadying the other cases with my other hand careful not to make the others tumble down. I placed the suitcase on the floor and clicked it open and found composition journals filled with my poetry from years ago. I opened the red composition journal and started reading. I smiled. I cried. I couldn't believe I wrote the poems from inside the blue suitcase when I was eleven.

I stumbled upon a poem: "If Heaven Had a Mailbox".

If Heaven Had a Mailbox

If Heaven Had a Mailbox...

I would write and ask my Mother

How she is each and everyday,

And if Heaven Had a Mailbox,

She could then reply and

Let me know if she's doing okay...

If Heaven Had a Mailbox...

Not only to my mother would I send a letter,

I would also write my Godmother asking,

"is Heaven a lot better?"

If Heaven had a mailbox...

I would send a tape recorder

To hear my mothers voice,

I miss her sometimes,

Why she's up there?

I wish was my choice.

If Heaven had a mailbox...

It would wash

all of my worries away

And finally release

All of this pain trapped inside,

From time to time I contemplate

How long this feeling of "loss"

Will continue to thrive

The loss is so alive that I think

I'm dying inside

If Heaven did have a mailbox…

I would finally be able to write

Happy Mother's day

Inside of a card,

The fact that Heaven

Doesn't

Makes my life and other

Lives hard.

I remembered why I wrote that poem. I reminisced to a very hard mother's day that my eleven year old self had had that year. In school, we were making paper mache vases for our mothers. I chose blue and purple tissue paper: my mom's favorite colors.

I pulled an empty clean spaghetti jar off the shelf and got to work piecing each paper thin scrap of paper on the jar with white globs of glue. Before it even dried I took out a permanent marker and wrote M-o-m in cursive. As I wrote M-o-m in cursive the teacher observed and asked with a troubled look, why I was making the gift for my deceased mother. I responded by telling her I was going to place it on her grave. The teacher replied by saying how I should make one for my guardian who now took care of me daily and that the tissue paper would wash away in the rain anyway.

As an adult, I'd imagined that I most likely turned red as a child as I recall the feeling I got that day. After school, I went home and thought about all the things I should have told that teacher: the biggest being curs(ive) kind of words. Then I wished my mom was there. Then I wished that Heaven had that dial up aol kind of internet service that the 90's had at the time.

Then I wished I could escape the very bad nightmarish dream I was kind of living in. I say kind of because I was becoming an existentialist at the age of eleven. I was living to exist. I mean I was writing lines like: I feel like I'm a slippery towel about to fall off the rack and a lot about death. People may label that as depression but there was nothing depressive in my mind about it. I missed my mom. Mom died=a lot of emotions at once. My hero died=intense disbelief accompanied by intense sadness accompanied by not wanting to tell a soul because who in the [expletive] could understand. As an adult, I don't understand.

I thought a lot on that day the teacher said the glued on tissue paper would just wash away in the rain anyway. Then I wished that Heaven at least had a mailbox. I was taught that you only have one mother and one father. Guardians don't count or can ever replace your real mother.

What would have happened if I wrote my mom that letter. After reading my poem, I put all of my poetry away and started writing a letter to Heaven now seventeen years later. I hoped it wasn't too late. At twenty six, "What will happen if it gets to Heaven?", I wondered.

Dear Mom,

I woke up today on a Sunday November 17, 2013, seventeen years later still missing you. I always felt that you were ok. I know in my heart, brain and soul that all is well. But I miss you even more than I did the day you left. I thought with time I would be ok. And, I am just that ok. But it doesn't stop the fact that I miss your presence. I miss you being here.

I am sending this first letter in hopes of a reply. I need you to know just how much we miss you and I don't care if this sounds so selfish but you need to know that. I have so much to tell you and I am sure it's likewise with you. I don't want to say too much in this first letter. I have so much to say that I feel overwhelmed with information but I don't want to overwhelm you. I love you more than everything in this universe.

Love, your daughter xoxoxoxo

Before sealing the letter into an envelope I prayed over it and wished it reached its final destination.

Waiting is the hardest part of all of this. Days, weeks, months later. Heaven does not have express mail or internet. After work one night, I drove home. Traffic. Waiting. Lights. Red lights. A thirty minute commute now one hour and thirty minutes.

I finally pulled up my street and parked in front of my brick apartment.

I took out my keys, I chose the small silver one and put it into a lock and turned it clockwise and opened the little silver panel door to find nothing. Not a single lick of mail. I took a deep breath. God she is in Heaven right?

    Everyday for months same routine: Pull up, park. Turn small silver mail key clockwise to find bills, junk mail. Sift through the mail. Throw the junk away.

One night pulled up. Paralleled park. Tripped going up the steps. Almost forgot to check the mail. Turned around. Walked up to the little silver panel door. Inserted small silver key, turned clockwise. I saw an unrecognizable letter. Pulled it out. Tore it open. I scanned the letter like it was in code until my eyes reached its special offer, "Send in for your free prayer cloth today!" I ripped it up in half.

I turned and walked up the stairs and took out the larger silver key and put it into the doorlock, turned it counterclockwise. I opened the door. I walked inside to cold air and a scent of cigarettes.

I closed the door and walked over to the thermostat and turned the heat on. I took off my coat and hung it up in the closet. I stood on tiptoes and reached for the dangling light switch cord to click it on. I turned on the fluorescent light and saw her.

My mother materialized before me. I rubbed my eyes. There she was, her back to me sipping on coffee and smoke rising above her head. Blueish hues mixing with grays, steam, haze and fog. I rubbed my eyes. My eyes burned. Unreal. *Am I going crazy?*

Before I said anything she spoke. Her voice, that raspy hoarse voice I have not heard in for…forever. "I got your letter". She placed her cigarette on the ashtray. "I have it with me". Then she reached for the letter and held it up. She turned to face me.

Tears fell from my eyes. My vision blurred.

"What are you waiting for?" She asked. She held out her arms. I ran towards her and embraced her. I cried. The letter crumpled. The letter was nothing. The letter was nothing compared to this moment. My mother let it drop to the ground.

"I can't take it with me anyway when I return" she said.

I could not find the words to speak. My throat was so sore. No one was going to believe this shit.

"What made you write?" asked my mother.

"I missed you."

"God had a lot to say about your little idea. And, insisted he just had to show you that anything is still possible". I smiled. How I wished that was true in her fighting cancer. I said that exact phrase to her when she was on her hospital bed so many years ago as she tried to explain what was happening to her body to my then ten year old brain. I wanted to be right in so many ways when I said, "Anything is possible".

As she spoke, her breath smelled like cigarettes and coffee. I missed this, I thought.

"You can't tell anyone about this" my mother said.

I started wondering what would

happen if I did.

Made in the USA
Middletown, DE
20 September 2019